P9-CFF-363

Dream Flights
on
Arctic Nights

Written by
Brooke Hartman

Illustrated by
Evon Zerbetz

ALASKA
NORTHWEST
BOOKS®

Text © 2019 by Brooke Hartman
Illustrations © 2019 Evon Zerbetz

Edited by Michelle McCann

Library of Congress Cataloging-in-Publication Data

Names: Hartman, Brooke, author. | Zerbetz, Evon, 1960- illustrator.
Title: Dream flights on arctic nights / by Brooke Hartman ;
    illustrated by Evon Zerbetz.
Description: [Berkeley] : Alaska Northwest Books, an imprint
    of Graphic Arts Books, [2019] | Summary: Illustrations and
    rhyming text reveal a child's dreams of flying over the Arctic
    and seeing the animals that live there.
Identifiers: LCCN 2018017241 (print) | LCCN 2018023312 (ebook) |
    ISBN 9781513261904 (ebook) | ISBN 9781513261898 (hardcover)
Subjects: | CYAC: Stories in rhyme. | Arctic regions--Fiction. |
    Animals--Arctic regions--Fiction. | Flight--Fiction.
Classification: LCC PZ8.3.H2574 (ebook) | LCC PZ8.3.H2574 Dre 2019
    (print) | DDC [E]--dc23
LC record available at https://lccn.loc.gov/2018017241

Published by Alaska Northwest Books
An imprint of Graphic Arts Books

GRAPHIC ARTS
BOOKS®
GraphicArtsBooks.com

Proudly distributed by Ingram Publisher Services.

GRAPHIC ARTS BOOKS
Publishing Director: Jennifer Newens
Marketing Manager: Angela Zbornik
Editor: Olivia Ngai
Design & Production:
    Rachel Lopez Metzger

Printed in China
22 21 20 19 1 2 3 4 5

At night,
just as the moon climbs high,
I make a wish that I can fly.

A raven clacks its inky beak,

And ruffles feathers, dark and sleek.

"Come quick!" it calls. "It's time to go."

Where will it lead? Perhaps you know.

Against my cheeks the north winds nip,

As fast along the earth we zip,

Across the land and over seas

To find new friends among the trees.

A pack of wolves on midnight prowl
Look up and give a welcome howl,
While ptarmigan and porcupines
Nod hello through the snowy pines.

The wolverines and grizzly bears
Give chase to shrews and
    snowshoe hares.
And owls hoot from spruce so tall,
"Who-hoo, who-hoo is there?"
    they call.

With eagles on the wind I soar

High over river, lake, and shore,

Past salmon swimming in a stream,

Their silver scales in starlight gleam.

Across the mountains topped with snow,
Still farther, farther north we go.
I call to mountain goats and sheep,
Who greet us with a daring leap.

With a puffin as my guide,

High up above the sea I glide,

Past beaches made of glacier clay

Where walrus, gulls, and sea lions play.

Near rocky shores, a raft of otters
Splash and dive upon the waters,
Fetching meals of clams and fish,
A baby otter's favorite dish!

Beneath the churning ocean foam,
The narwhals and belugas roam,
While bowhead whales breech and sing
And flap their fins like mighty wings.

A snowy owl with feathers white
Flies me deeper through the night,
Across a frosty tundra plain
To lands where ancient glaciers reign.

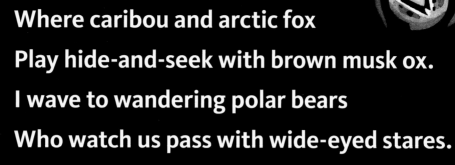

Where caribou and arctic fox
Play hide-and-seek with brown musk ox.
I wave to wandering polar bears
Who watch us pass with wide-eyed stares.

Suddenly, the sky ignites
In streaks of green and golden lights!
The colors flicker, dart, and play.
"Come dance with us!" they seem to say.

Then like the flash of rainbow trout,
One by one, the stars wink out.
Knowing night is soon to end,
I say goodbye to my new friends.

On rustling wings, so swift and black,
My raven comes to guide me back.
Then as the sunrise streaks the sky,
Away to home we turn and fly

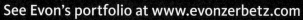

Brooke Hartman is an Alaskan mom, wife, and national award-winning author of books for children. She writes from her home in Chugiak at the base of the mountains that inspired this story and many others. Follow her Alaskan writing adventures on Facebook at @BrookesBooksAK.

Evon Zerbetz is an Alaskan artist who has illustrated books for children including *Blueberry Shoe*, *Ten Rowdy Ravens*, and *Little Red Snapperhood*. Her linocut constructions and public art installations are installed in public buildings throughout Alaska. Evon works in her studio over the ocean, on the island community of Ketchikan.

In her most recent flying dream, she flew a plane through the clouds to a remote island in the Alaskan rainforest. When she realized she didn't know how to fly a plane, she then flew home with her own superpowers. She learned to fly in her dreams by hopping.

See Evon's portfolio at www.evonzerbetz.com